# THE SCENT OF BLOOD

Tanya Landman is the author of many books for children, including *Waking Merlin* and *Merlin's Apprentice, The World's Bellybutton* and *The Kraken Snores, Sam Swann's Movie Mysteries: Zombie Dawn!!!* and three stories featuring the characters Flotsam and Jetsam. Of *The Scent of Blood*, the fifth title in her award-winning Poppy Fields series, Tanya says, "I used to work in a zoo full of hungry – potentially man-eating – carnivores. When I started writing, it seemed a perfect place to set a murder mystery."

Tanya is also the author of four novels for teenagers, including *Buffalo Soldier*, which won the Carnegie Medal, and *Apache*, which was shortlisted for the Carnegie Medal and the Book Trust Teenage Fiction Prize. Since 1992, Tanya has also been part of Storybox Theatre. She lives with her family in Devon.

You can find out more about Tanya Landman
and her books by visiting her website at
**www.tanyalandman.com**

527 512 79 2

Poppy Fields is on the case!

*Mondays are Murder*
*Dead Funny*
*Dying to be Famous*
*The Head is Dead*
*The Scent of Blood*
*Certain Death*
*Poison Pen*
*Love Him to Death*
*Blood Hound*
*The Will to Live*

Also by Tanya Landman

*Waking Merlin*
*Merlin's Apprentice*
*The World's Bellybutton*
*The Kraken Snores*

For younger readers

*Flotsam and Jetsam*
*Flotsam and Jetsam and the Stormy Surprise*
*Flotsam and Jetsam and the Grooof*
*Mary's Penny*

For older readers

*Apache*
*The Goldsmith's Daughter*
*Buffalo Soldier*
*Hell and High Water*

# THE SCENT OF BLOOD

TANYA LANDMAN

WALKER
BOOKS

This is a work of fiction. Names, characters, places and incidents
are either the product of the author's imagination or, if real, are used
fictitiously. All statements, activities, stunts, descriptions, information
and material of any other kind contained herein are included for
entertainment purposes only and should not be relied on for
accuracy or replicated, as they may result in injury.

First published 2010 by Walker Books Ltd
87 Vauxhall Walk, London SE11 5HJ

This edition published 2013

2 4 6 8 10 9 7 5 3

Text © 2010 Tanya Landman
Cover illustration © 2013 Scott Garrett

The right of Tanya Landman to be identified as author of this
work has been asserted by her in accordance with the
Copyright, Designs and Patents Act 1988

This book has been typeset in Slimbach

Printed and bound in Great Britain by Clays Ltd, St Ives plc

All rights reserved. No part of this book may be reproduced,
transmitted or stored in an information retrieval system in any
form or by any means, graphic, electronic or mechanical,
including photocopying, taping and recording, without prior
written permission from the publisher.

British Library Cataloguing in Publication Data:
a catalogue record for this book is available from the British Library

ISBN 978-1-4063-4719-7

www.walker.co.uk

*For the Marvellous Maggie and for Chris,*
*my very own walking encyclopedia*

GRAMPIAN *Zoo had closed to the public half an hour ago. Director Dougal McTaggart leant back in his office chair. He loved this time of day. It was as though every single creature let out a simultaneous sigh of relief once the gates clanged shut. He heard the keepers calling goodnight to each other as they headed home for tea. He should leave too, but first he'd take one last stroll through the grounds. He enjoyed having the place to himself.*

*He had stopped to watch the chimpanzees when his walkie-talkie crackled into life. A desperate voice could be heard pleading, "Help! I need help! Is anyone there? Oh, please..."*

*"Chris?"*

*"Yes!"*

*"Where are you?"*

*"With Alisha! It's... She's... Help! Please help me!"*

*Dougal McTaggart didn't wait to hear more. He sprinted down the path towards the elephant house.*

*The door was wide open. Inside, Alisha, the old cow elephant, was calmly scratching her giant buttocks against the rough surface of the far wall. The zoo director could see Chris's booted legs behind her. The keeper was pinned against the stonework.*

*Dougal didn't phone for help. He needed to act, now. He leapt the barrier, then squeezed between the* iron bars. He fished the remains of a chocolate bar from his pocket, held it up and called the elephant's name.

Alisha lumbered forward, allowing Chris to fall to the ground. Taking the chocolate delicately in the tip of her trunk, the elephant eyed the zoo director thoughtfully before transferring it to her mouth. He edged around her vast bulk towards the unconscious figure. But when he got closer he recoiled in shock. It wasn't Chris – it was a shop dummy! What was going on?

Then he heard a movement behind him. A voice giving a word of command. Obediently Alisha lifted her trunk in salute and stepped smartly back. This time it was the zoo director who was caught against the wall. But he was no plastic mannequin. The sheer weight of the cow elephant cracked his ribs one by one. As the life was squeezed out of him, someone began to laugh. Malicious. Vengeful. Cruel. It was the last sound Dougal McTaggart ever heard.

# TYGER, TYGER, BURNING BRIGHT

MY name is Poppy Fields. I'm not a huge fan of the Animal Kingdom. It's not that I don't like the natural world – if a wild creature stumbles across my path, I'm quite happy to look at it for as long as it wants to hang around. But if there's a choice between watching some*one* and watching some*thing* I'll usually opt for some*one*. Which turned out to be a big mistake when Graham and I visited the zoo. If I'd paid more atten-tion to our furry friends I might have prevented several beastly murders.

It was a few weeks after Easter. Graham and I were back at school and nothing exciting seemed likely to happen any time soon. But then Mum announced that she'd won first prize in some charity raffle: a long weekend break for a family of four at Farleigh Manor Zoo. Mum rang to explain she was the single mother of an only child and they said we could each bring a friend. So she invited her best mate, Becca, and I invited Graham. The zoo booked us in for the May bank holiday weekend, and at the crack of dawn on the Saturday morning we set off.

Farleigh Manor had once been a stately home set in hundreds of acres of private parkland. You know the kind of thing – a sweeping driveway and huge lawns kept manicured by gazillions of gardeners; vast staircases and elegant rooms with massive chandeliers and gleaming silverware kept polished by armies of maids. A rich businessman had bought the whole estate from an impoverished aristocrat a while ago. Peter Monkton had made his fortune by manufacturing dodgy fast food with names like Chicky Chunkies, Beefy Blocks and Duckie Dazzlers. When he'd hit sixty-five he'd retired to Farleigh Manor and put his feet up. He'd wanted to live the quiet life of an English country gentleman, but he got bored stiff within a year. So he ended up stuffing the grounds with wild animals and turning the place into a tourist attraction. He did a good job of it – the place became really popular with families who wanted a good day out, and pretty soon he was getting thousands of visitors a year. But then Peter died and his son, Anthony, inherited the lot.

Anthony Monkton was what my mum called "eccentric" and Becca called "barking mad". To be honest, some of what he did sounded pretty bizarre. Graham had printed off reams of information that he'd found on the Internet (he likes to be prepared for things), so we looked through it on the way up. The first thing we noticed was that Anthony Monkton had a distinctive taste in clothes. There were several pictures of him swanning about in brightly coloured kaftans. He sported a pointy beard at least fifteen centimetres long and a ludicrously extravagant moustache that was waxed into lethal-looking spikes at each end. Apparently he was fascinated by New Age philosophies, and freely confessed to sleeping in a pyramid-shaped tent that he'd erected in his private apartments, claiming it gave him a "mystical energy". He had recently started adding his own touches to Farleigh Manor. First of all a series of yurts – big, domed tents – had sprouted like mushrooms on the front lawn, where people could try out alternative therapies to Rebalance their Karma. Then he'd gone even further and converted the west wing of the manor into the Healing Harmony Hotel and Spa. It was newly opened, so the raffle prize had been part of a publicity stunt to attract customers. Mum – who'd recently been attacked by a mad, drill-wielding workman – said that a dose of highly concentrated rest and relaxation was just what she needed. She and Becca were planning to try out all the facilities on offer. Meanwhile, Graham and I were having three days Behind the Scenes with the keepers, getting a chance to meet some of the animals up close and personal.

I had to admit that the idea of combining a health spa and a zoo was totally weird. Anthony Monkton had to be a genuine, real-life eccentric. I couldn't wait to meet him.

It was a long drive to Farleigh Manor, and we'd set off so early that before long I started to doze. By the time Mum pulled up outside the front entrance I was deeply asleep. Being woken up by a load of angry shouting came as quite a shock.

I opened my eyes to see a group of about fifteen people bunched around the barrier by the ticket office, stopping us from going in. They were waving placards furiously, and one of them crashed his into our windscreen so hard that I thought he might crack the glass. Just in case we couldn't read them for ourselves, they were all shouting their slogans at the tops of their voices.

"Keep Wild Animals in the Wild!"

"Free the Captives!"

"End This Imprisonment NOW!"

Mum wasn't pleased, but Becca was positively irate. She wound down her window and said acidly to the leading protester, "You're blocking our way. That's illegal."

The protester – a ferret-faced man of about thirty – came right back with a caustic remark of his own. "You're going in there," he said in a strong Scottish accent, pointing through the gates. "That's immoral."

"Oh, for heaven's sake! We can't be doing with all this. We're just here for the weekend. Move out of the road or I'll call the police." Becca pulled out her mobile and started tapping the keys. The ferret-faced man lowered his placard and backed away reluctantly.

"Anthony Monkton should be locked up in a cage!" he yelled at Becca.

"You tell her, Christopher!" a girl protester egged him on.

"Give him a taste of his own medicine!" added another.

"Exploiting innocent animals to line his pockets. He's evil!" screamed a fourth. "And you lot shouldn't be supporting him!"

Complaining loudly, the protesters huddled together like extremely bad-tempered sheep as Mum accelerated towards the ticket office.

"Bunny huggers," the man in the glass booth

grumbled, jerking his thumb towards the mob. His name tag declared him to be Ron Baker. "Sorry about them. They've been at it for months. You'd think they'd have better things to do with their lives."

"We won the raffle," Mum told him by way of reply. "We're staying for the weekend. The booking's in my name. Lili Fields?"

The man consulted his computer screen. "Oh yes. The Healing Harmony Hotel and Spa," he said, and his lip curled into a slight sneer of disapproval. "Follow the drive to the house and take the right-hand fork. You'll find the entrance in the courtyard to the rear of the building. Enjoy your stay, Ms Fields." He didn't sound at all convinced that we would. He pressed a button, the barrier lifted and Mum drove through, away from the noise of the protesters' chants. For a while I could still see their faces in the wing mirror. The ferrety guy – Christopher – looked like he was boiling with furious thoughts. Hatred oozed from every pore – you could see it in the hunch of his shoulders, in his tightly clenched fists – and I felt a sudden prickle of apprehension. Was it just my imagination, or did he look like he could do someone some serious damage?

As we drove through the grounds I had the distinct impression that the zoo had seen better days. I'd had a quick look at the map that Graham had printed off, so I knew it was divided into four themed areas: the African Savannah, the Rainforest, the Australian Outback and the Frozone, where they kept animals from the icy poles. From what I could see through the car window, the enclosures seemed nice and big and the animals looked well fed and cared for – but the signs were faded, the paint was chipped, and weeds grew in cracks in the paths. The whole place felt kind of unloved. Neglected. As if the person in charge had his mind on Higher Things. Then we got our first glimpse of the house – an amazingly grand mansion that was somehow totally eclipsed by the brightly coloured flags flying from the crop of domed yurts that dotted the grass in front of it. You could tell at a glance where Anthony Monkton's heart lay.

The manor's huge south-facing façade looked out over the yurt-strewn lawn, and on either side – propping it up like a pair of bookends – were two long, rather less impressive wings. We turned right along the side of the east wing, where Anthony Monkton had his private apartments, and came to an arch that led through to an enclosed, rectangular courtyard. The west wing – where the spa was housed – was opposite us when Mum parked. The fourth side, on our right, comprised a coach house (now the education centre) and stables (now the zoo stores). The offices were on the left, in the basement that had once been the servants' quarters.

Mum's plan was to check in and deliver our gear to our rooms, then she and Becca would go for a sauna while Graham and I wandered around the zoo. We weren't due to meet our first keeper until 11 a.m. so we had a bit of time to explore on our own.

But as soon as she switched off the engine and we all climbed out of the car, we found ourselves right in the middle of another drama.

The office staff had obviously only just arrived for work. Two smartly dressed women in high-heeled shoes were standing on the cobbles looking perplexed. Behind them were three zoo keepers, distinguishable by their matching wellies and overalls. All five staff were staring at the back of the house.

REMEMBER S.M.? had been sprayed across the wall in big block capitals with blood-red paint.

Graham and I exchanged a quick, curious glance.

"S.M.?" I heard one of the women say. "What does that mean, Angie?" The person I assumed was Angie seemed equally mystified. She didn't answer.

I looked beyond her to the keepers. A blonde twenty-something-ish girl with her hair scraped back into a ponytail had her hand to her mouth. Behind her was a stick-insect-thin man of about the same age, and beside him stood an older guy who'd grown a massive beard to make up for his baldness but unfortunately had ended up looking as if his head was on upside down. Physically they were all totally different, yet there was something oddly similar about them. I stared for a few seconds, trying to work out what it was, then realized with a jolt of surprise that it was the expressions on their faces. While the office staff were puzzled and unsure what to do, the keepers were looking... What? My eyes flicked from face to face. It was the strangest thing. They weren't happy; they weren't pleased. They were *satisfied* – as if the right thing had finally been done.

Just then, another keeper – whose name tag helpfully declared him to be Charlie Bales – came through the archway with an empty wheelbarrow, obviously heading towards the stores. When he saw the writing, he stopped, and the same look of grim satisfaction spread across his features. He nodded his head as if in approval.

"S.M.," he said, dropping the barrow's handles. "Well, well, well." He looked at the assembled crowd and asked, "Anyone told our glorious leader?"

They all shook their heads but said nothing. Charlie Bales pulled a walkie-talkie from his top pocket and pressed a couple of buttons.

"April? It's Charlie. Could you tell Mr Monkton that someone's sprayed some graffiti out here?"

We could hear April relate the message to her boss in a broad Birmingham accent. There was a grunt of alarm – the sound of a man who'd rather not be bothered by the real world.

"You can deal with it, can't you, April?" a timid voice protested. "Can't you get someone to wash it off? What's the man called? Jerry, is it? That chap in the maintenance department. Get him to do it."

"April, tell Mr Monkton it's not the protesters' usual stuff," Charlie said calmly. "This is on the wall of the house. I think he should take a look. This message seems ... personal."

"What does it say?" asked April. Charlie read out the words loud and clear. They were met with a long silence. Then April said to her employer, "I suppose you'd better have a look, sir. It won't take a minute." There was the sound of a chair being pushed back. Two minutes later, Anthony Monkton joined us in the courtyard with his secretary.

The sight of a man in a flowing yellow kaftan and purple beret was every bit as bizarre as I'd hoped. He looked as if he was wearing a nightie. His unruly grey hair poked out from the beret like a collection of rodents' tails – rats trying to desert a sinking ship, I thought. He wore a necklace with a large crystal dangling from it, which he clung to with one hand as if it would give him magical protection.

It was the first time I'd ever been in close proximity to a genuinely eccentric person. I was gripped – and I wasn't the only one. Every single member of staff stiffened and pulled themselves up a little when he appeared. Shoulders went back, chins were raised. It was almost as if they were standing to attention. But then I noticed that what showed in their eyes wasn't respect. It varied from person to person, but I saw traces of pity. Disappointment. Dislike. And – in Charlie Bales's face – open contempt.

Mr Monkton looked at the writing while the keepers looked at him, waiting for his reaction. Their boss rummaged in the pockets of his kaftan for his glasses. Once he found them he gave them a rub with a hanky before putting them on his nose. Eventually he said, "I don't understand. S.M.? Who...?"

There was a tense silence. Every staff member apart from April wore the same expression. Disgust.

At last Charlie Bales spoke. "Sandy," he said. The name seemed to thud onto the cobblestones.

"Sandy?" echoed Mr Monkton, baffled. "Sandy who?"

The female keeper gasped. Pain flashed across her face. The stick insect next to her scowled at his boss.

"Sandy Milford." Charlie's voice was quiet but deadly.

And yet Mr Monkton seemed entirely unaware of their seething emotions. His face contracted into a tight frown and he said vaguely, "Sandy Milford? The keeper who…? Oh dear… Yes, of course. Terrible thing. Very sad. Tragic." A nerve twitched in his cheek. "April, sort it out, will you? Wash it off, or paint over it or something. I'll be in my office if anyone needs me." He took off his glasses but didn't move. It was as though he couldn't quite remember where his office was.

April came to his rescue. "Let's go inside, shall we, sir?" She looked at the others. "Come on, everyone," she said briskly. "Back to work. Mr Monkton doesn't pay you just to stand around."

Dismissed, the staff left the courtyard. Then April's eyes fell on Mum and Becca standing uncertainly by the car. "Can I help you?" she asked.

"Oh!" Mum looked flummoxed for a moment. "Er – we're staying in the hotel. We won the raffle."

"Ah, yes. Congratulations. Ms Fields, isn't it? You'll find the reception area through those double doors. Enjoy your stay."

April pointed across the courtyard, then turned to lead Mr Monkton away.

It was only then that we realized someone had crept quietly up behind us. Someone who was now staring at the graffiti, a wide, toothy grin fixed in a striped orange and black face.

It was a tiger.

Or at least it was someone in a tiger suit – bright, fuzzy and fake.

But Anthony Monkton reacted as if he'd come face to face with a man-eating killer. His glasses dropped from his hand, the lenses smashing on the cobbles. And then he screamed.

# SANDY MILFORD

MR Monkton's scream echoed across the courtyard, bouncing from one wall to another, high and ear-piercingly loud. The tiger ripped off its head to reveal the flushed face of a young woman whose hair was dyed almost as orange as the suit she was wearing. "I'm so sorry, Mr Monkton!" she gabbled. "I didn't mean to scare you! Are you all right?"

Faces had begun to appear at the basement windows, peering up at their boss in astonishment, and Mum and Becca were staring at him with their mouths open.

"Where did you get that?" April demanded. Her hands had bunched into fists and for a second I thought she might actually hit the girl.

The tiger-lady pulled at her fur. "This? It was on my desk. There was a memo attached. I thought you..."

April interrupted her roughly. "For pity's sake, Zara, haven't you got anything better to do than fool around in fancy dress? Go and get changed."

April moved away, steering Mr Monkton down the stairs to the basement offices.

Graham and I were left standing beside Zara.

"But I *haven't* got anything better to do," she told us forlornly. "I'm supposed to keep the kids happy. It's what I get paid for." She sighed, replaced her head and stomped across the courtyard dejectedly, her long stripy tail trailing behind her. She disappeared into the education centre and there was a moment's pause before Mum, looking slightly apprehensive about the weekend ahead, said, "Let's go and get checked in, shall we?"

The Healing Harmony Hotel and Spa had the hushed, reverential atmosphere of an old-fashioned museum or library, or maybe even a Buddhist temple. It was all polished wood, slate and empty white walls. Wind chimes tinkled gently every time a door opened or closed, and the staff spoke softly, as if scared of disturbing the meditative atmosphere. Mum and Becca couldn't wait to get on with some serious rest and relaxation. As soon as we'd dumped our bags in our rooms, they both disappeared in search of Mystical Energy, leaving Graham and I to explore. After collecting our information pack from the receptionist, we headed out across the courtyard. A man – presumably Jerry from the maintenance department – had already begun to wash the blood-red paint off the wall.

"Remember S.M.," I said. "Sounds threatening, doesn't it?"

"It does have a rather menacing tone," agreed Graham.

"Sandy Milford," I mused thoughtfully. "You wouldn't need to remember him unless he wasn't around any more, would you?"

"No," said Graham. "That seems to be a fairly safe assumption."

"So he's probably dead. And as Mr Monkton said it was 'tragic', I think we can assume he didn't die of old age." I looked at Graham. He was trying to avoid meeting my eyes. "We can't ignore it," I told him. "We're going to have to find out what happened."

Gleaning information about Sandy Milford proved surprisingly easy. The Great British Public were out in force, so there were plenty of people milling around. As far as the staff were concerned, Graham and I were just like every other punter – i.e. totally invisible. Which provided us with plenty of opportunities for eavesdropping.

Everyone who worked in that place seemed to love a good gossip, and the people who had seen the graffiti before it got scrubbed off were having a great time telling the people who hadn't. For the next hour or so, wherever we went we heard the events of the early morning being told over and over again. In the shop, in the café, by the burger bar – if two members of staff were standing together, they seemed to be having pretty much the same conversation. Each one was marked by the same ghoulish relish, and they all went something like this:

"In blood-red paint, it was. 'Remember S.M.?'"

"Sandy Milford?"

"Who else?"

"Who did that, then?"

"No idea."

"Poor Sandy. It was a shocking waste, really it was. No one should die like that."

"Killed by a tiger!"

"Horrible!"

I glanced at Graham. He looked a little pale.

"It's his kiddies I feel sorry for. Poor loves."

"And his wife."

"Mr Monkton was pretty upset when he saw it."

"Serves him right. There are plenty of people around here who think it was all his fault. He just hasn't kept up with things the way his father did, has he?"

"He screamed!"

"He never!"

"Yes, he did."

"Why?"

"That new girl came up behind him. What's her name? Zara. She was in that old tiger outfit."

"I thought they got rid of that after the accident. Didn't April say it was bad taste to keep it?"

"That's what I heard. God knows how she ended up wearing it."

"Someone's idea of a joke?"

"Reckon so. It made Mr Monkton nearly jump out of his skin. Silly sod. Everyone in the office saw him."

A heavy bout of sniggering brought each conversation to a close.

"They don't seem to like Mr Monkton much, do they?" I said to Graham.

"No... And yet the man seems harmless enough," he replied.

"Maybe that's the point. I mean, you wouldn't want someone harmless in charge, would you? You'd want someone who could do the job." I thought back to the days when my mum had worked for the Town Parks Department. She'd complained endlessly about her boss because he wasn't "up to it". She'd left in the end and set up her own landscape gardening business, saying she'd rather live with her own mistakes than someone else's.

"You could well be right," mused Graham. "I read an article recently about what voters expect from their leaders. Charisma, intelligence, charm. They like a certain commanding presence; a superior quality. I suppose there's no point following them otherwise."

"Well, Mr Monkton certainly doesn't seem to tick any of those boxes," I said. "Maybe that explains why he's not popular. And if he's not running the place as well as his dad did, no wonder people are moaning."

By 10.45 a.m. Graham and I knew that Sandy Milford had been a keeper who'd been killed by a tiger about a year ago, but we were no closer to knowing who'd sprayed the graffiti on the wall. And by then we were due to start our fun-filled schedule of Organized Activities.

"We'd better get going, I suppose," I said, checking my watch. "Where exactly are we heading?"

Graham pulled out the information sheet the spa receptionist had given him. "According to this, we have to meet by the door marked 'Staff only', which is right next to the proboscis monkeys' enclosure."

"Funny name for a monkey," I remarked.

"Proboscis means nose or snout," Graham informed me. "I believe the males' noses are particularly pendulous. They can grow up to eighteen centimetres long."

It's fantastically useful having a walking encyclopedia for a best friend. "I bet you memorized the map, too. Where do we go?"

"This way," he said.

"And who are we meeting?" I looked over his shoulder at the neatly typed schedule and my mouth dropped open. We were spending the morning with someone called Kylie Milford! I pointed at her name and nudged Graham.

"Well, this is going to be interesting," I said. "She's got to be related to Sandy, hasn't she?"

Graham looked at me and nodded. "I'd have thought it was highly likely. There would seem to be two possibilities. She's either the dead man's sister ..."

I finished his sentence for him. "...or she's his wife."

# HOT AND HUMID

WHEN we arrived in the Rainforest, the proboscis monkeys were all lined up on a branch fast asleep. Graham was right – even the females had ridiculously large noses, which dangled from their faces like water-filled balloons. The door marked STAFF ONLY was slightly ajar, and through it we caught a glimpse of the keeper we'd seen in the courtyard that morning. She was attacking a pile of fruit with a gleaming knife, chopping it into tiny pieces with savage relish. We stopped in our tracks.

"Do you think that's Kylie?" I asked nervously.

"Could be."

Before we could take another step, the stick-insect

man loped past us, pushed open the door and went inside. As one, Graham and I glided towards it like shadows, hoping to catch a bit of their conversation.

"Feeling better now, Kylie?" he asked her.

"A bit, yeah. Thanks, Pete." She sniffed and blew her nose. "It's silly, me getting so upset. It's just seeing that writing brings it all back. I'm hardly likely to forget Sandy, am I? I think about him every day. Every minute. He's always there, in my head. And when I think of the kids...!" She started crying and Pete patted her awkwardly on the back as if he didn't quite know how to comfort her.

He tried to lighten the mood by saying, "Hey! At least it gave old Monkton a nasty shock. Did you see his face? I thought he was going to die!"

"I wish he would." The bitterness in Kylie's voice made Pete drop his arm and take a step back. "He deserves to. We all know what happened. That stupid judge can blame Archie Henshaw until he's blue in the face. We know whose fault it really was. Look at what he's done to this place! The man's a joke. He deserves everything he gets."

She attacked a melon, splitting it in two with a single blow. Pete flinched and hurriedly changed the subject. "You doing the Behind the Scenes stuff with those kids today, then?"

"Yes." She checked her watch. "They ought to be here by now. I hate it when people are late." She glared towards the door and, desperately hoping she hadn't noticed us eavesdropping, I knocked on it to announce our arrival.

Kylie made no attempt to explain the red-rimmed eyes or pink-tipped nose that clearly showed she'd been crying. Instead she got straight down to business. First she gave us a Health and Safety talk, then we had to don the matching green overalls she handed us, and after that she took us off to the "jungle". She was pretty much running on automatic pilot, giving the same tour she'd obviously given to loads of kids before us, but I still found it interesting. The problem was, we couldn't quite bring ourselves to ask her what we really wanted to know: just how, exactly, was she related to Sandy Milford?

The first animals she introduced us to were a pair of Brazilian tapirs – furry pig-sized creatures with what looked like miniature trunks. We watched them over the barrier for a moment or two before Kylie announced that we were going in. I have to confess I was a bit nervous. I couldn't help wondering how big their teeth were, and Graham looked as though he might refuse altogether. But I took a deep breath and did what I was told, and when Kylie instructed me on where to scratch them (right between the shoulder blades), to my surprise they became absolutely blissed out. First their eyelids started to flutter and then their little trunky noses went all floppy. Then their knees gave way, and finally they sank to the ground with a contented sigh and literally rolled over.

"Brilliant!" I said.

"Extraordinary." Graham flashed me one of his blink-and-you-miss-it grins.

"Works every time." Kylie threw a quick smile at the animals.

After that it was time to feed the spider monkeys, who came right up to the wire mesh to take pieces of banana from us with their delicate, bony fingers. Then Kylie took us to a little private room behind the enclosure. In a small cage on the table, a tiny snub-nosed proboscis monkey clung to a large furry teddy bear.

"This is Basil," she announced, her face softening with almost maternal pride.

"What's the teddy bear for?" I asked.

"He needs something to cuddle when I'm not here," she explained. "He was rejected by his mum so I've been hand-rearing him."

"I understand that's a terribly demanding task to undertake," said Graham. "From what I've read, it seems to be extremely hard work."

"Yep, it's pretty tiring. This little fella needs feeding every two hours, night and day. He comes home with me every evening. I haven't had much sleep lately – but he's worth it, aren't you, baby?"

She began to warm his bottle.

"What will you do with him?" I asked as she fed him.

"Oh – he'll go in with the others when he's old enough. I'll keep a careful eye on him, but he should be fine."

I touched the fur on the top of his head and felt the heat through his paper-thin skin and the tiny, rapid beat of his pulse. "You must be really attached to him," I said. "Won't it be hard giving him back?"

"Of course. But he's a wild animal, not a pet. You can't go getting sentimental over them." When Basil had finished his bottle, Kylie lifted him into his cage and he climbed into the welcoming arms of his teddy-bear foster mother. "Anyway," she added, "he doesn't belong to me. I don't get any say in the matter." There was a touch of anger in her voice so I didn't ask any more, and then she told us our next stop was the tigers.

"We're not going in with them, are we?" quavered Graham.

"Yes," said Kylie.

I gulped. "Is that safe?" I could barely squeeze the words out.

She laughed. "Don't worry." She led us to a huge pair of wooden gates that were big enough to drive a lorry through. A small, person-sized door was cut into the corner of one, which Kylie opened. "This is the service area," she said as we followed her inside. "The bit the public don't get to see."

It was a small concrete yard. Cages with old-fashioned iron bars lined the walls. They were linked by heavy mesh tunnels with sliding gates at each end.

"We'll get the tigers shut in here first, then we can go in to the public enclosure. We've had new doors fitted recently: there are at least four of them between you and the tigers. You'll be fine." Kylie slid open the one to the public enclosure and whistled. Like trained circus animals, three tigers responded to her summons. With practised ease she threw each one a small piece of meat, and before I'd had a chance to see what she'd done with the gates and tunnels, she had each of them safely contained in separate cages. Even though my conscious mind told me there were iron bars and bolts between us and them, I still experienced a clutch of panic. They were so big. So powerful. I thought of Sandy Milford and felt faint.

"They must be very dangerous," I said weakly.

"All animals are dangerous if you don't respect them," Kylie replied shortly. She thrust a shovel towards me. "Hold that."

Graham looked as pale as I felt, but Kylie was unsympathetic. She shoved a broom into his hand, dropped a sack of meat into a wheelbarrow and, grabbing its handles, told us to follow her. Before long we found ourselves in the tiger enclosure with the Great British Public on the other side of the glass, gawping and making sarcastic remarks like "Funny-looking tigers!"

"That one's got no fur."

"Oi! I paid to see animals, not a pair of kids. I want my money back."

Kylie ignored their witticisms and led us over to where a wooden pole was sticking out of the ground, as thick and as tall as a tree trunk. Opening the sack of meat, she spiked a large piece with a lethal-looking hook and proceeded to hoist it to the top of the pole on a rope and pulley.

"What are you doing?" Graham was intrigued.

"It's called environmental enrichment," explained Kylie. "Keeps them busy. They have to climb if they want to eat. It makes them work for their food in the same way as they would in the wild."

"Ingenious," Graham commented approvingly.

When Kylie finished with the meat, she pulled a bottle of aftershave from her pocket. Strangely, mystifyingly, she began to pour it into various holes drilled in the pole. "They like different smells," she told us curtly. "I vary what I pour in from day to day. It stops them getting bored."

When she'd emptied the last drops from the bottle, she turned to me and Graham looking faintly amused. "Now it's your turn," she said. "Time to do the mucking out."

Tiger poo is very big and very smelly. By the time Graham and I had shovelled the last of it gingerly into the wheelbarrow, our eyes were watering and we were both feeling slightly queasy, despite the fact it was nearly lunchtime.

When we'd finished the job to Kylie's satisfaction, she led us back out and performed the reverse manoeuvre with the safety gates. The three tigers sort of flowed with brutal grace back into their outside enclosure.

"That's your lot, then," she said briskly. She made no attempt to disguise the fact that she was glad to be getting rid of us at last. "I've done my bit. You're in the Frozone this afternoon, aren't you?"

Graham didn't need to check our schedule. It was

already imprinted on his super-retentive brain. "Yes."

"OK, then. Bye." Kylie turned to go. We were dismissed.

It was now or never. "It must be a difficult job looking after tigers," I blurted out. "People must get hurt every now and then, however careful they are."

"Well, yes." Kylie gave me a hard stare. "Tigers sometimes kill their keepers. But the most dangerous animal in captivity is the elephant."

"Really?" Surprise threw me off my line of questioning. "I thought elephants were quite docile. People ride on them all the time in India, don't they? I've seen it on TV."

"True. But they kill more keepers than all the other animals put together. The director of Grampian Zoo was crushed to death last year. Sometimes I think..." She broke off, but her eyes had narrowed and her expression had become intense and ruthless. I could almost see the thought rising like a bubble from her head.

Kylie Milford was fervently wishing that Anthony Monkton had suffered a similar fate.

# CREEPY-CRAWLIES

I felt a bit shaky after we'd mucked out the tiger enclosure. I couldn't decide which I'd found more frightening: the animals or Kylie. She was like a volcano, simmering with heated anger. What would it take to make her erupt?

We had an hour free before we were due in the Frozone, so Graham and I bought ourselves a burger and Coke each and settled down on a bench overlooking the waterhole in the African Savannah. It had been cleverly designed so that the meat-eaters were separated from the vegetarians by moats, electric fences and the occasional see-through barrier. From where we were sitting it looked as if they were all together on the grassy plain: lions, hyenas, zebras, hippos, rhinos, elephants and giraffes. But it was the same here as in the rest of the zoo: the signs were peeling and faded, the glass unwashed, the bench cracked and wobbly.

"So…" I began. "That graffiti means that someone's trying to upset Mr Monkton. They blame him for Sandy's death. Especially Kylie."

"That seems to be an accurate summary of what we've heard so far," agreed Graham.

"I tell you what, though. The timing's a bit odd."

"What do you mean?" he asked.

"Well, if the accident happened a year ago, why wait until this morning to spray graffiti on the wall?"

Graham sipped his drink. "Kylie mentioned a judge. As you know, in cases of accidental death there has to be an inquest. There must have been some sort of inquiry, but these things can take months. It might only just have been completed."

"What difference would that make?"

"It's conceivable that the graffiti artist was hoping to obtain what they considered to be justice through the official channels. If Mr Monkton was cleared of all blame, that person might have been provoked into taking matters into his or her own hands."

I was impressed by Graham's reasoning. "OK," I said. "That sounds about right. Kylie seems convinced it was Mr Monkton's fault, doesn't she? And as far as we know, lots of people agree with her. Who was that other man she mentioned this morning – Archie Henshaw?"

"Yes." Graham nodded. "If we could get access to a computer we could probably find out who he is. But I don't see how we can manage that just now."

I drained my Coke and then said, "I tell you another weird thing about this morning. That girl Zara turning up and freaking out Mr Monkton. Didn't someone say that the tiger suit had been got rid of?"

"Yes."

"They also said she was new, so she can't have known about it. Someone deliberately put it in her office." I crushed my Coke can between my palms and threw it into the recycling bin. "I wonder if we can talk to her."

After we'd eaten, we walked back towards the manor house in search of Zara. She wasn't hard to find: she'd ditched the furry outfit, but her dyed orange hair was as bright as a Belisha beacon. We could see her from way across the front lawn, sitting in an open-sided yurt surrounded by a sea of Brownies. When we got closer, we realized she was doing a hands-on creepy-crawly session. Or at least she was trying to. Her audience was a little on the excitable side, wriggling around on the benches like an infestation of yellow maggots. There was a load of giggling and shrieking and girls-being-girlie-girlie over the insects, and even though she was using a microphone, Zara's voice was too weak to cut through it.

"What I'm going to show you next is a special kind of insect all the way from the rainforests of Madagascar," she said, her eyes widening in an attempt to convey the Marvellous Miracles of Mother Nature.

"Where's that?" demanded one Brownie.

"Er... It's near Africa. They're quite big – when they're adults they can grow to about eight centimetres. They're excellent climbers and can even walk up a sheet of glass."

"Big deal," said another Brownie witheringly, and the girls either side of her giggled.

Zara took out a box labelled MADAGASCAN HISSING COCKROACHES and the squealing reached a new intensity. One of the Brownies chose that moment to jump up, hands clapped over her mouth as if she was about to be sick. Brown Owl reacted like greased lightning, whipping out a paper bag and clamping it to the unfortunate girl's mouth. But in doing so she caught Zara's elbow and the box of cockroaches went flying.

Fifteen large cockroaches landed on the heads of fifteen small Brownies. The girls leapt hysterically off the benches, flapping at their hair and flicking the insects to the floor. The poor bewildered cockroaches scuttled in all directions. Zara tried frantically to retrieve them, but she didn't have enough hands to scoop up more than one or two before the Brownies stampeded from the yurt. When the last of the yellow-clad squealers had fled across the lawn, she looked ready to burst into tears. It was too good an opportunity to miss.

"Do you want some help?" I asked.

"Oh yes, please," Zara said gratefully.

So Zara, Graham and I spent the next twenty minutes rounding up hissing cockroaches.

There's something bonding about hunting creepy-crawlies, and we got quite friendly as we crawled under the benches together. Miraculously we managed to locate all fifteen, although I have to say that one or two looked suspiciously like common-or-garden pests rather than their exotic cousins. After they'd been safely returned to their box, Zara rewarded our efforts by buying us another Coke in the Ballroom Café.

"What a day!" she said. "And it won't be over until nearly midnight. I'm supposed to be a teddy bear at the staff party tonight. I'm entertaining the kids – and some of them are hideous." She looked at us, suddenly aghast. "Oh, whoops – your parents don't work here, do they?"

"No," I assured her. "We're visitors."

"Oh, right. Didn't I see you two first thing this morning?" she asked, opening her drink.

"Yes," I said, adding pointedly, "when you were in the tiger suit."

"That suit!" she exclaimed, banging her can down on the table so that the Coke frothed out. "That was so strange. Where did it come from? That's what I want to know."

"Do you?" I said as casually as I could manage.

Graham asked neutrally, "Why were you wearing it?"

Zara's brow furrowed. "It was in my office this morning with a memo from April – Mr Monkton's secretary – saying it was a replacement for the bear outfit. I have to dress as a teddy when we get big crowds in. It keeps the toddlers amused, you see."

"Right."

"But then April said she didn't write any memo. So someone must be playing a stupid practical joke," she said miserably. "Laughing at the new girl. I suppose they think it's funny."

"Any idea who?" I asked.

"No," Zara replied, sniffing. "It might be one of the keepers. Some of them have a very odd sense of humour."

"Maybe it was the same person who sprayed the graffiti on the wall?" I suggested.

"Do you think so? But I didn't understand that either. Who's S.M.?" Zara looked puzzled.

"We presume that he was the keeper who died last year: Sandy Milford," said Graham.

"Sandy Milford?" Zara echoed. "Is *that* who it's about?" She sat back in her chair and sighed. "I've heard people talking about him. His sister's one of the keepers."

"Kylie?"

"Yes, that's right. And Charlie Bales – Kylie's boyfriend – is his wife's cousin, I think."

"Really?"

"Oh yeah – and apparently his wife used to work here too, before she had kids. They all seem ever so close. That accident must have been really traumatic for everybody." Zara sounded wistful. Lonely. An outsider excluded from the pack. She finished her drink. "Better get back to work," she said. "I've got a session with the Cubs in a minute. I hope they're better behaved than the Brownies!" She flashed us an anxious grin and left, but her words hung in the air.

"Traumatic for everybody," Graham repeated thoughtfully.

"Yes," I said. "But is one of them traumatized enough to take revenge?"

# THE SCENT OF DEATH

AFTER the lunch break Graham and I made our way to the Frozone with a growing sense of unease. The animals seemed strangely tense too. As we walked past the Savannah the zebras kicked out at each other, ears laid back, yellowed teeth snapping. In the Rainforest the monkeys screeched and squabbled. Despite Kylie's effort with the log and the aftershave, the tigers paced restlessly.

"Do you reckon someone wants to hurt Mr Monkton?" I asked Graham.

"Statistically speaking, the writers of anonymous notes rarely resort to physical violence. I would assume that the same rule applies to graffiti. As we know, the object of the exercise is to terrorize the victim."

"Well, it worked. The poor man was scared stiff this morning. But who did it? It has to be an inside job, doesn't it?"

"I would have thought so," ventured Graham. "Mr Monkton certainly isn't popular with the protesters outside the gates, but it seems unlikely that they'd be concerned about the death of a keeper."

"And they wouldn't know the effect the tiger suit would have, either, would they?"

"No," Graham agreed. "Which all points to the culprit being a member of the zoo staff."

We were due to meet our next keeper at 2 p.m. by the polar-bear pit. At five to two we were both standing there watching the animals dozing on a concrete rock.

"I don't know," I said, surveying the enclosure. "You can't help feeling that those protesters might have a point. It's not exactly the Arctic wilderness, is it?"

"It's a complex ethical issue," Graham replied sagely. "If global warming continues at its present rate, a zoo might be the only alternative to extinction."

We didn't have time to debate the matter any further, because just then Charlie Bales appeared, clocked our green overalls and said, "You're the Behind the Scenes kids, right?"

We nodded.

"OK. Follow me."

Kylie's manner had been brusque, but Charlie's was positively menacing. The first thing he did was take us into the little kitchen near the polar-bear pit. Reaching up to a high shelf, he pulled down two small bottles and gave one to each of us. They were the old-fashioned sort – square-based, heavy, with a large glass stopper – the kind of thing you might see in a Victorian chemist's or a Mad Science Lab. Mine was half full of clear liquid. There was no label telling me what it contained.

"Have a sniff of that," he urged me. "Go on. Take a deep breath."

I didn't like the way his eyes were glinting, but I couldn't think of any reason to refuse. Hoping it might be aftershave, I pulled out the stopper and did what I was told.

It was only with a monumental effort that I managed to stop myself emptying my lunch and breakfast and everything else I'd ever eaten onto the tiled floor. I have never, ever smelt anything so utterly stomach-churningly disgusting. It literally made my head reel and I had to sit down on the nearest chair to recover.

Charlie Bales laughed nastily, and Zara's words about keepers with an odd sense of humour drifted through my head. I'd have bet all my pocket money that he'd been the one to put that suit in her office.

I couldn't speak, but Graham – who'd caught a whiff even though he hadn't breathed it in – said faintly, "What *is* that stuff?"

"Putrescine," said Charlie.

"Putrescine?" echoed Graham. "As in *putrid*? Meaning rotten? Decomposed?"

"You've got it."

Graham and I exchanged a worried glance. We were at the mercy of a total madman. Graham's solution seemed to be to keep him talking until we could escape.

"But why…?" he began.

"The bears love it," said Charlie. "I soak logs in it from time to time. Keeps them very busy, it does…" He leant forward until his nose was almost touching Graham's. "It's the scent of death."

"Environmental enrichment?" Graham's voice wavered back at him.

"You're learning," said the keeper gruffly.

"And what's this one?" Graham asked politely, holding up the bottle Charlie had put in his hand. I noticed he was careful not to remove the stopper.

"Cadaverine," Charlie answered promptly.

"As in cadaver? Corpse?"

"Yep."

"Ingenious." Graham was rapidly running out of conversation ideas. "Very clever. Lovely. Hmm…"

There was a short silence. I was still feeling too sick to speak, but fortunately Charlie decided he'd had enough of his little joke. He took the bottles from our unresisting hands and put them back on the shelf.

"I won't be giving them either of those today," he said, winking at Graham. "You're off the hook. They had all they needed to eat this morning. You can help me with the penguins instead."

Feeding the penguins was fun. They were all different shapes and sizes, from the king penguins, that came up to my waist, to the little rockhoppers, that barely reached my knees. One was really tame and waddled along behind us, taking fish from our hands. After that we got to feed the fur seals, so all in all our afternoon with Charlie proved a lot more enjoyable than we'd expected at the outset.

Our Behind the Scenes tour ended at 4.30 p.m. and just as we were washing our hands in the kitchen, April appeared and said to Charlie, "Mr Monkton wants you to sort the bears out before tonight." Without even glancing at us she added, "Give them a scatter feed. Throw in a couple of logs, too – he wants them kept busy this evening."

A look of irritation passed across Charlie's face. "They were fed this afternoon," he said, glancing pointedly at his watch. "I haven't got anything prepared."

"Well, prepare something now, then," April said brusquely. "They'll be disturbed by the party and Mr Monkton doesn't want them pacing. It might upset the hotel guests."

"I finish work in half an hour," Charlie protested.

"You'd better be quick, then, hadn't you?" replied April coolly. "Mr Monkton can't afford to pay you overtime. And he'll be down to check on them before the party, so don't take any short cuts."

April walked away, oblivious to the furious glare Charlie Bales was burning into her back. Graham and I finished washing our hands, muttered a quick goodbye and slipped out of the kitchen as fast as we could. Just as we were closing the door, Charlie's walkie-talkie crackled into life.

"You nearly ready to go?" a woman's voice asked.

"No," he replied sourly. "Sorry, Kylie."

"Oh, OK. I'll get a lift home with Angie, then."

"You better had. I'll be stuck here now until the party. April's just said Monkton wants me to feed the bears again."

"What, now?" Kylie sounded as angry as Charlie.

"Yeah. Just throw in a couple of logs, she says."

"Like you can buy them in the supermarket!" Kylie sighed. "That man's got no idea, has he?"

"Well, I hope I don't see him before the party, that's all I can say. The way I feel right now, I might just do him an injury."

I looked at Graham. He pursed his lips. We didn't like the sound of that at all.

# RED IN TOOTH AND CLAW

GRAHAM and I returned to the Healing Harmony Hotel and Spa. It wasn't until we walked in and noticed the other guests looking at us with horrified disapproval that we realized quite how much we stank. What with the tiger poo, the putrescine, the dead fish and the penguin droppings, we weren't very nice to know. The receptionist pressed a hanky over her nose and mouth as she handed us the keys to our rooms. When we banged on Mum's door to let her know we were back, she took one disgusted sniff and ordered us both to take highly scented bubble baths.

When we were thoroughly clean and had changed into fresh clothes, dropping the overalls in the hotel laundry for sterilization, we discussed the plan for the evening. Mum and Becca had been massaged to within an inch of their lives and were in favour of supper followed by an early night.

"I've never felt so tired in my life," said Mum. "All this relaxation? It's exhausting!"

It turned out that the hotel restaurant only did light high-vitamin-super-detox-low-calorie-gluten-free vegan and vegetarian meals. Mum and Becca didn't mind, but Graham and I had been working pretty hard all day and wanted something more substantial than a tofu and tomato wrap.

"You could try the Ballroom Café," the receptionist told us. "The annual staff party's in there tonight but I'm sure they'll be able to find you something if you go across now. I'll let them know you're on your way."

So Graham and I left Mum and Becca nibbling carrot sticks and crossed the courtyard to the manor house.

Preparations were already well under way for the evening, but the kitchen staff were really nice to us. They loaded up two plates with piles of macaroni cheese and baked beans left over from lunchtime and handed us bowls crammed with fruit salad. We tucked ourselves into a corner next to the gents' toilet. Instinctively I'd picked a table behind a huge potted plant, where we'd be out of the way. Although we were almost completely hidden, we had a good view of the ballroom, the entrance hall and – through the window – the whole of the front lawn.

We hadn't even started on the pudding when Mr Monkton, smartly dressed in a conventional black suit and tie, came down the sweeping staircase. April, in a flowing apricot dress, was beside him. She looked cool and confident; he looked pale and troubled. They stopped at the bottom of the steps and she adjusted his bow tie.

"Why am I doing this?" we heard him groan. "I don't like parties."

"It's traditional," replied April, picking fluff off his lapel. "Your father always did it. It's what the staff expect."

"Do I have to give a speech?"

"Yes, dear. Nine-thirty as usual. It doesn't have to be a long one."

"But I don't feel like it," he complained. "And after this morning they'll all be laughing at me."

"Of course they won't," soothed April.

"I dream about it, you know. All the time. I can still see the tiger's eyes. I wish I hadn't given that order."

"Don't think about it, dear. Not now. You'll only upset yourself."

There was something strange about the way April

was speaking to Mr Monkton, but I couldn't quite put my finger on it. Then the staff started to arrive and I became distracted. First abandoning their kids to Zara in the yurt, they came into the entrance hall to shake hands with their boss.

We could see Zara through the window, dressed in a teddy-bear suit, trying to keep the first few arrivals happy. She wasn't doing a very good job of it. As we watched, one of them kicked her in the shins and another tried to rip her head off. She hung on to it as if her life depended on it.

"I don't much fancy her chances of survival this evening," I murmured to Graham.

Just then a ruddy-cheeked man in excessively shiny shoes strode into the hall and shook Mr Monkton firmly by the hand. He looked as if he didn't recognize the new arrival for a moment. Then April whispered something in his ear – presumably a name – and he said, "Mark! How nice to see you. How are you?"

"Fine," Mark replied energetically. "How's that monkey's abscess? Want me to come and check him over tomorrow?"

April stepped in. "No, I'm sure that won't be necessary," she said, smiling politely. "We can't have you billing Mr Monkton for extra visits. Not at the fees you vets charge these days! You can check him over when you come on Monday, as usual."

"Fingers tightly on the purse strings, Anthony – just what I like to see!" Mark guffawed, his ruddy cheeks wobbling like the wattles on a rooster. "That's the way to keep the place turning a profit." Slapping Mr Monkton hard on the back, he came into the ballroom and sat himself down at a table.

Not long afterwards, a group of keepers arrived. If she hadn't been with Charlie and the stick-thin Pete, I wouldn't have recognized Kylie. She was dressed in a midnight-blue satin dress and her blonde hair was loose about her shoulders. She looked stunning. Charlie Bales, on the other hand, was in the jeans and T-shirt he wore beneath his overalls. April looked at him disapprovingly.

"Didn't have time to go home," Charlie said pointedly in response to her unasked question. "And I'm not missing tonight for anything."

The keepers took the drinks the waiters offered and then sat down at the table nearest to Graham and me. Perfect, I thought, hoping to overhear some tasty morsels of zoo gossip. But they didn't say much that was interesting. The talk was all about who was going out with whom or whose kids were going through a difficult phase or what TV programmes they'd watched lately. Everything they discussed seemed bland and neutral, and I began to wonder if they were deliberately guarding their tongues. The more I watched them, the more they looked like actors going through their lines. Yet underneath the tight, polite conversation their eyes seemed bright and alert as if they were suppressing their excitement. Was it the result of that morning's events? Or was something about to happen?

The staff party consisted of a big, sit-down meal followed by a bit of dancing. By the time we'd finally finished our pudding, their first course had arrived and Graham and I were kind of trapped in our corner. We couldn't get out without having to squeeze between the tightly packed tables, so we stayed put. They started serving the meal just before eight o'clock and the keepers tucked into their first course with relish. But at about ten past eight Charlie Bales suddenly got up and rushed to the gents', where we heard him being violently sick.

I was about to comment on it to Graham when I noticed Mr Monkton answering his mobile phone. He was sitting at the far end of the room, so I couldn't hear his conversation, but his face suddenly clouded with confusion. He said something to April and then left.

The second course arrived and Charlie Bales hadn't returned. Graham went off to the loo, and when he came back he said Charlie was still being sick.

When Kylie had finished her food, she leant over to Pete and said, "I'd better go and feed Basil. He'll be hungry by now."

"I'll come too," he volunteered, and they both slipped outside.

"Charlie had better watch out," the bearded Mike Hobson said with a broad wink to his wife, and there was a smattering of laughter from the other keepers. "Looks like he's got competition for Kylie's affections."

Outside, things seemed to be going from bad to worse for Zara, who was now being chased in large circles around the lawn by a pack of screaming infants. I watched for a bit, wondering if we should do anything, when Mike decided to nip out to check on his kids.

Everyone but Charlie was back at the table when the puddings arrived, and then the waiters brought coffee. At about 9.15 p.m. Charlie finally emerged from the gents' and slumped onto a chair next to Kylie.

"You all right?" she asked.

"Been better. Must have been something I ate."

"Shall I take you home?"

"Yeah," he nodded. "But we'd better listen to Monkton's speech first. You know what he's like. He'll be in a right huff if we walk out before he's done his famous last words."

When the clock struck the half hour Jerry from

maintenance switched on the microphone at the top table, which let out a squealing whine. Everyone turned to the front, ready to hear Mr Monkton's speech.

But Mr Monkton was nowhere to be seen.

April looked flustered. "He's not answering his phone," she hissed at Jerry, but her words were caught by the mike and broadcast across the ballroom. "He said someone told him there's a problem with the bears. I'll go and see what's keeping him."

The ballroom fell silent for a moment, then there was an excited buzz of chatter at the unexpected drama.

Something awful had happened. I was one hundred per cent certain of it. I looked at Graham and he nodded. We broke cover, pushed our way between the tables and headed for the door.

So we were the first ones to see April stagger back across the grass a few minutes later, her face drained of all colour, unable to speak.

We were the first ones to sprint in the direction in which she was pointing. Towards the Frozone. The polar-bear pit. Where we found Mr Monkton. Or what was left of him.

And we were the first ones to read the words that had been chalked on the path: S.M. WILL BE AVENGED!

# THE BEAR FACTS

THE police talked to us right after they'd finished taking a statement from April, who was weeping uncontrollably. We were horribly shaken up too: the polar-bear pit hadn't been a pretty sight. I mean, Graham and I had seen plenty of dead bodies before, but nothing quite as gruesome as that.

But if we were upset, Mum was almost beside herself. After the rigours of all that intense relaxation, she'd fallen fast asleep. She'd had no idea we'd been at the party until the police woke her up to be the Responsible Adult at our interview. She was horrified about us getting involved in yet another murder investigation.

Graham and I knew how to stick to the facts. We

didn't offer a single opinion. We'd learnt from experience that policemen aren't keen on hearing unproven theories from a pair of kids. Not that we really had any theories at that point – there was way too much we didn't know.

"I'll probably need to talk to you again," said Inspector Murray, the policeman, once we'd finished. "You're staying here in the zoo hotel, aren't you?"

"Yes," said Mum sadly. "We're supposed to be having a nice, relaxing weekend break. Some hope."

"Good," he said briefly, ignoring her tone. "I'll be in touch again in the morning."

As soon as the inspector left, Graham and I were ordered to our rooms and given strict instructions to go straight to sleep and not stir until the morning. Mum went to bed and fell into such a deep slumber that I could hear her snoring from across the corridor. It was pretty late by then, but I couldn't sit still – my mind was buzzing with everything we'd seen and heard that day. Graham must have been the same, because about five minutes after Mum crashed out there was a faint tap on my door and he was there, his eyes shining with excitement. It turned out that what I'd taken to be a flat-screen TV in the corner of my room was actually a computer. All the rooms had one, and Graham had just discovered that the hotel gave free Internet access. Which meant we could start trawling for information straight away.

We began with Sandy Milford, typing his name into the search engine, but we didn't learn much more than we'd already overheard. Sandy – the father of two children – had been killed a year ago when a tigress broke through her cage door. Charlie Bales had been part of the emergency response team and had rushed to his aid. He was quoted as saying tearfully, "I tried to save him. But I was too late."

The accounts that had appeared in the press were very sad, but not exactly news as far as we were concerned.

Then I thought of looking up Archie Henshaw and things suddenly got much more interesting.

The first thing we found was his obituary. Archie had jumped off a bridge the week before. It turned out that he had worked in the zoo's maintenance department.

"So there *was* an inquiry into Sandy Milford's death," said Graham, pointing at the screen. "I was right. Look – it says that it reached its conclusion a week ago. The judge found Archie Henshaw to be negligent." He read aloud, *"Zoo director Anthony Monkton produced documentary evidence in the form of a series of memos detailing work to be done. Archie Henshaw – for reasons he was unable to explain satisfactorily – ignored the direct instructions of his employer. He was consequently relieved of his post."*

I whistled through my teeth. "So he got sacked, and then he killed himself? Poor man!"

We sat looking at the screen in silence for a few moments, digesting this new information. And then I said, "I don't get why Kylie blames Mr Monkton for the accident if it was Archie's fault."

"It does seem a little illogical," Graham agreed.

There was another pause. As we sat there, the vision of a grinning tiger suddenly flashed through my mind. Bright orange. Synthetic fur. Plastic teeth. I was tired by then – overtired, I thought – I must be going slightly bonkers. But then I realized the significance of the tiger suit.

"You can fake memos," I said suddenly. "Someone did it to Zara this morning!"

Graham stared at me. "You think Mr Monkton might have provided forged evidence to the court?"

"It's possible, isn't it?"

"I suppose so. But it would be terribly unethical." Graham looked outraged.

"What if he made up all that documentary stuff?" I asked.

"He might have done. But why would he neglect the fabric of the buildings?" Graham was perplexed. "Even if he deceived the judge to save his own reputation, surely a responsible zoo owner wouldn't knowingly put his staff in danger in the first place?"

"Come on, Graham, you saw him in action today!" I said. "He was more interested in alternative therapies than the animals, let alone the people who worked for him. He didn't even remember who Sandy was! And the whole of the zoo is run down. I bet that's why the keepers blamed him for Sandy's death." I was pacing now, up and down the room, trying to work things out. "OK, so our murderer's got to be someone who knew Sandy. Agreed?"

"Agreed." Graham nodded.

"So that rules out anyone who joined the zoo in the past year."

"And the office staff," added Graham. "That girl – Angie – she didn't understand the meaning of that graffiti, did she? Neither did the other one."

"No... But that's a bit odd, because didn't Kylie say she was getting a lift home with Angie? You'd think if they were that friendly she'd know about Kylie's brother. She might have been pretending she didn't. Still, it was more likely to have been one of the keepers. Which one, though? It can't have been Charlie, can it?"

Graham shook his head firmly and shuddered. "No – he was far too unwell."

"But Kylie and Pete left to feed Basil, so they could have done it. Mike, too – he went out to check on his kids." A thought suddenly occurred to me. "Of course it doesn't *have* to have been one of the keepers. Jerry put the microphone up just after nine, but he wasn't in the room before then, was he? And he would have worked with Archie. He must have been furious that Archie got blamed for the accident if it wasn't really his fault. And then with Archie killing himself... That would give him a really good motive."

"True," said Graham.

"I don't think April could have done it, though," I decided. "She was so upset."

"She did appear to be terribly distressed," agreed Graham.

The thought flashed through my head that there was something strange about April, but I still couldn't pin down what it was. "She was his secretary," I said slowly. "She must have done all his typing. So if he had forged that evidence, she'd have known, wouldn't she? And yet she didn't say anything. So she's got to have been on his side." I breathed out and sat back down in a leather armchair, suddenly exhausted. "Zara said the keepers are a really close-knit group, but that probably applies to the other departments too. As far as I can see, pretty much everyone in the zoo had a motive for wanting him dead."

"Yet Mr Monkton was only out of the room for half an hour," said Graham reasonably. "Most of the staff were present in the ballroom for the entire time – we saw them ourselves. It should be a relatively straight-forward matter for the police to work out who had the opportunity to commit the crime."

But sadly it turned out not to be quite as simple as Graham had thought. When Inspector Murray arrived at the hotel the following morning, we told him which keepers had left the ballroom. But he informed us that none of them had gone anywhere near the Frozone. Kylie and Pete had fed Basil – Jerry had seen them and so had the guy from the ticket office, Ron Baker. Mike had gone to check on his kids, but Angie had done the same, so they could vouch for each other.

Their alibis slotted together like pieces of a jigsaw puzzle. Neat. Tight. A perfect fit. Almost as if they'd been planned.

# EAVESDROPPING

FARLEIGH Manor Zoo was closed to the public the day after Mr Monkton's murder: firstly so that the police could search the grounds, and secondly as a mark of respect. But the animals still needed feeding and cleaning out, so the keepers turned up as usual. Graham and I could hear the protesters yelling at them as they arrived for work. The ferret-faced Christopher's Scottish accent rose above the others as he called out, "Jailer!" and "Torturer!"

We weren't due to meet Mike Hobson for our Behind the Scenes tour of the African Savannah until 11 a.m. Mum and Becca were determined to achieve as much Serious Relaxation as they could possibly squeeze in, so after breakfast Graham and I wandered off into the grounds for a spot of investigating. The trouble was that with no Great British Public milling about, we stuck out like sore thumbs and our opportunities for eavesdropping were severely limited. Groups of staff who had clumped together for a good gossip melted away like snow in spring when they saw us coming. Very frustrating. The only person who seemed even remotely pleased to see us was Zara, who'd come in to feed the education centre's animals.

"Oh – hello, you two," she said with a faint smile. She sounded completely and utterly dejected. "I thought you'd have gone home by now."

"No," replied Graham. "We're staying the weekend."

"So you were here last night?"

"Yes," I said.

"Crikey!" Zara rolled her eyes. "Those kids! Just as well I'm a fast runner. It was a complete nightmare. I could have been killed!"

As soon as the words were out of her mouth Zara flushed scarlet. "Whoops! I shouldn't have said that. I forgot about Mr Monkton for a second. Bad taste. Sorry."

"Speaking of bad taste," I said, changing the subject, "Do you think it could have been Charlie Bales who put that suit in your office?"

Zara looked at me, eyebrows raised in sudden realization. "Yes! It could have been, couldn't it? Charlie's got a really weird sense of humour. He's forever playing jokes on people. One time he made me sniff one of those bottles of stuff he keeps for the polar bears. I nearly passed out."

"He did that to us, too," I said.

"Did he? That's the kind of thing he finds funny. It's sick, really. Yes, I bet it *was* him." There was a pause and then she said, "I've got to feed the cockroaches and things. Then I might as well be off home, I suppose. I was meant to be doing a session for the St Mary's Sunday School outing but everything's been cancelled. Oh, well. At least I don't have to face any more kids today." She smiled weakly and went on her way, leaving me and Graham with plenty to talk about. We meandered towards the proboscis monkeys' enclosure, finally coming to rest on a bench that was half hidden by a clump of bamboo. Kylie was in the kitchen, chopping fruit again. We tucked ourselves into the vegetation so that she wouldn't be able to see us but we would still be able to hear if anything interesting happened.

"Charlie Bales," I said softly. "I think we ought to keep an eye on him."

"He couldn't have done it," said Graham firmly.

"He was vomiting the entire time. It would have been physically impossible."

"OK, but I reckon he definitely did the thing with the tiger suit. He could have done the graffiti, too, couldn't he? He was the one who called Mr Monkton on his walkie-talkie. He wanted to make sure his boss saw it."

"He might well have wanted to unsettle his employer," Graham conceded. "But it doesn't necessarily follow that he planned his murder."

"Maybe not. But he was really angry about having to do those logs for the polar bears and then not having time to go home and get changed before the party."

There was something else about that whole business – something that was tickling away at the back of my mind. I frowned in concentration. "Graham," I said at last, "you know when April came down to tell Charlie to sort out the bears?"

"Yes…"

"Didn't he say he'd fed them already?"

"Yes, I believe he did. In fact, as I recall, his exact words were: 'They were fed this afternoon.'"

"Then he was lying!" I said triumphantly. "I mean, we were with him, weren't we? He didn't give them anything. In fact, he told us he'd fed them in the morning. But suppose he hadn't…?"

"What are you suggesting?" asked Graham.

"What would have happened if the bears had been really hungry?" I demanded.

"Two ravenous carnivores?" Graham replied thoughtfully. "I'd have said it offered an extraordinarily efficient way of disposing of a body."

"So if April hadn't come down... If Charlie *hadn't* fed them... Mr Monkton might never have been found! Those bears wouldn't have left a shred of evidence."

We stared at each other, aghast, and for a few seconds we were completely silent. Which was just as well, because at precisely that moment Charlie Bales himself decided to pop in for tea and biscuits with Kylie.

"There *is* justice in the world after all," he told her, not bothering to lower his voice as he pushed open the door to the kitchen. "Put the kettle on, love, and crack open the chocolate biscuits. Let's celebrate. Our glorious leader has finally got what he deserved."

*"Shh!"* Kylie hissed urgently. "What if someone hears you? You shouldn't say stuff like that!"

"Come on, Kylie, you didn't like him any more than I did. Think of what he did to Sandy! Archie, too, for that matter. He got what was coming to him."

"Maybe," Kylie conceded. "But you shouldn't say it. Not now. Keep your mouth shut. The police..."

Charlie interrupted her with a scornful grunt. "The police are useless around here. They couldn't even track down a stolen bike, I reckon. Trust me, Kylie, they'll never work it out."

"They were here in the kitchen this morning, asking about that old tiger suit."

Charlie stiffened. "Did you tell them anything?"

"Of course not. But someone will. You should never have taken it out of that bin."

"Maybe. Maybe not." Charlie sniffed dismissively. "It was just a joke. It doesn't mean anything."

Kylie chopped away in silence for a few moments. Then she said, "That policeman said he was stabbed. Lots of times." Her voice rose higher.

Beside me, Graham gave a sharp intake of breath. My mouth fell open.

"That's what they told me, too," said Charlie casually.

"Inspector Murray said that some of the wounds were really deep. But others just glanced off his ribs." Kylie looked up at him miserably. "Who killed him, Charlie?"

Charlie laughed. "We'll probably never find out who struck the fatal blow. Pity, really. I'd like to shake the killer by the hand." His words sent a shiver down my spine. Draining the dregs from his mug, Charlie kissed Kylie goodbye and walked away.

Between the bamboo leaves, Graham and I watched him swagger jauntily down the path.

For someone who had spent the previous evening heaving his guts up, he looked surprisingly perky.

# THE AFRICAN SAVANNAH

GRAHAM checked his watch. It was almost time to meet Mike Hobson. Once Charlie was out of sight we freed ourselves from the bamboo and headed through the Frozone towards the African Savannah. According to our schedule we'd be meeting the giraffes, mucking out the zebras and feeding the baby elephants.

"What did Kylie say yesterday?" I asked Graham nervously. "Isn't the elephant the most dangerous zoo animal of them all?"

"That's what she said," he replied, his voice wobbling just a little. "But surely their calves shouldn't prove too much of a threat?"

We stopped and looked at each other uncertainly.

"I suppose there's only one way to find out." I shrugged, then changed the subject. "Charlie seems to have recovered from his illness very quickly, doesn't he?" I said.

"Yes, he does. But I believe that would be consistent with mild food poisoning."

"Mmm... I'm not so sure. I reckon he might have been faking."

Graham frowned, puzzled. "I can't see how he'd have managed it. We both heard him, didn't we?"

We'd reached the penguin pool by now, and at precisely that moment Charlie came marching breezily up the path, whistling and swinging a bucket of sardines in each hand. He acknowledged us with a brisk nod as he let himself into the enclosure. An eager rockhopper waddled towards him and he threw it a small fish. There was no escaping it: Charlie looked healthy. Robustly healthy. Suspiciously healthy.

An idea began to take shape as we walked on. As soon as we were out of earshot I said urgently, "No one went to check on him last night, did they? And we didn't actually *see* him. We just heard him being sick, that was all."

"What do you mean?"

"Pop singers mime along to their songs sometimes, don't they?"

"True." Graham nodded solemnly. Last Christmas we'd been tricked by someone doing just that.

"Could Charlie have been using a recording?" I asked. "He might have gone into the toilet, switched on the player, rung Mr Monkton on his mobile to get him to go to the bear pit, then climbed out of the window. He could easily have stabbed Mr Monkton, then got back in without anyone knowing."

"It's technically possible for him to have broadcast the sound of vomiting," said Graham slowly. "There are all kinds of ways he could have done that. But there was the smell, too. It was vile when I visited the gents'. It's a very distinctive aroma."

"Yeah." I deflated instantly. "I don't see how you could fake that." We trudged on through the Frozone, past the little kitchen where Charlie had almost made me keel over the day before. In my head a great big light bulb suddenly lit up. "Those bottles!" Stopping dead, I stabbed a finger at Graham's chest. "Putrescine! Cadaverine! Suppose Charlie's got one in there that smells like puke?"

"What a dreadful thought!" Graham exclaimed.

"He could have, though, couldn't he?"

"Theoretically, yes. I suppose you could manufacture that kind of odour."

We both looked at the closed kitchen door.

"You're not suggesting we find out?" asked Graham weakly.

My legs felt wobbly at the very thought. I mean, I'd nearly passed out the day before. I wasn't exactly keen to repeat the experience. I took a deep breath. "Look, Graham," I said, summoning up my courage. "Charlie definitely did that thing with the tiger suit – he more or less admitted it back there. We know he hated Mr Monkton. He's *got* to be the killer. But if we're going to tell the police, we need proof. We've got to know if one of those bottles contains the scent of sick. We're going to have to sniff them."

Graham gulped and looked green about the edges and I felt exactly the same. We'd be late to meet Mike Hobson, but it felt like we had no choice.

Graham checked his watch. "It will take Charlie about ten more minutes to feed the penguins. We'd better be quick."

Seizing our opportunity, I turned the handle and opened the door, and together we sneaked into Charlie's kitchen.

A whole row of bottles lurked nastily on the top shelf. I took down the first and, holding it at arm's length, gingerly lifted the stopper a fraction. The ghastly aroma of long-dead fish wafted out. Hastily pushing the stopper back in, I replaced it on the shelf.

"OK," Graham croaked courageously, "I suppose it's my turn."

He took down the second bottle and raised the stopper no more than a millimetre. Weirdly, the smell of strong coffee filled the room.

"Lucky you," I grumbled, removing the glass stopper from the third. It was full of cheap aftershave. The next one stank of poo. Then it was wee. We worked our way along the entire shelf, feeling steadily more ill with each disgusting aroma. When Graham pulled the stopper from the very last bottle, the unmistakable scent of sick filled the room. Queasily triumphant, I looked at Graham. "Bingo! This is all the proof we need. We'd better find Inspector Murray."

Graham opened his mouth to reply. But before he'd managed to get a single word out, a gunshot rang across the grounds. Monkeys screamed in alarm. Tigers roared. Gulls took to the skies, shrieking.

And Charlie Bales fell face down into the penguin pool, stone dead.

# TEAMWORK

**S.M.** WILL BE AVENGED!

It was scrawled on the path beside the pool where Charlie Bales lay as dead as the fish he'd been throwing to the penguins. I dimly registered something odd about the choice of words, but in my shocked state I couldn't figure out what it was.

Inspector Murray arrived on the scene about two seconds after us. He took one look at the dead keeper and then ordered Graham and me to wait for him in the hotel. We sat in a dark corner of the lobby, muttering quietly to each other.

"Charlie's death has got to be connected with Mr Monkton's, hasn't it?" I said.

"Undoubtedly," agreed Graham.

"OK... Mr Monkton. Let's start with him. Inspector Murray didn't tell us about those stab wounds," I said resentfully.

"Perhaps he thought it was an unsuitable subject to discuss with minors," replied Graham.

"It sounds weird, though," I puzzled. "Some were really deep. You'd need to be pretty wound up to do that, wouldn't you? But others just glanced off his ribs. How could that happen? You'd have to have your eyes shut. Or not be trying hard enough." Another possibility suddenly hit me like a sledgehammer.

Different wounds.

Different blows.

Different hands holding the knife.

"Graham," I whispered, my eyes practically popping out of my head. "Suppose they *all* did it?"

"Who? What do you mean?"

"Well, we agreed that everyone had a motive even if they didn't have the opportunity, didn't we?" I said. "I reckon this is about justice. It's Payback Time for Sandy's death. And Archie's. Just like Charlie said. Mr Monkton was cleared of blame at the inquiry, so they all decided to kill him. Maybe everyone who left the room that night was involved: Charlie, Kylie, Pete, Mike, Angie, Ron. Jerry, too. That's why their alibis backed each other up – they'd planned it beforehand. One blow each. No one would know who struck the fatal wound. That's why Kylie asked who killed him and Charlie said, 'We'll probably never find out.' And if the original plan had worked, the bears would have eaten Mr Monkton and the police wouldn't have known he'd even been stabbed. It would have looked like an accident – like he'd fallen in or something."

"It sounds perfectly plausible," said Graham. "But where does Charlie's murder fit into this highly orchestrated scheme? Who killed *him*?"

I thought about Charlie. Loud. Breezy. Over-confident. "Mike said something about Pete being competition for Charlie, didn't he? Do you think Pete's in love with Kylie?"

"In the USA, love triangles are number seven on the list of most common reasons for murder," Graham informed me.

"Plus, Charlie couldn't keep quiet. Kylie told him to shut up but he wouldn't. He was really full of himself. He was putting everyone in danger."

"But why write those words on the path?"

"It must have been a diversion. As soon as Inspector Murray gets here, we'll tell him."

Mum had to be pulled out of a Seaweed Wrap treatment to attend our interview. She wasn't very happy about having to sit there plastered in green gunk wearing nothing but a dressing gown. We kept everything brief and to the point, but if the policeman was impressed by our theory, he didn't show it. He listened carefully and nodded thoughtfully before telling us, "I hate to disappoint you, but the keepers' alibis are absolutely watertight. Of course we'll check and double-check, that's routine police procedure. But I'm sure that none of them was involved."

When he'd finished with us, Mum disappeared back into the spa and the policeman went in search of keepers to interview. We were allowed to spend the rest of the day doing what we were scheduled to do with Mike Hobson, but he wasn't exactly welcoming. In virtual silence we fed the baby elephants – who turned out to be perfectly harmless and very cute. Then we visited the giraffes, who seemed to lower their heads out of the sky to take their bananas. Mucking out the zebras was hard work, so we didn't really have time to think or talk.

We finished at 4.30 p.m. again and went back to the hotel for another scented bath. The Ballroom Café was shut, seeing as the zoo hadn't been open to the public all day, so we had to chew our way though a couscous, halloumi and spinach salad in the hotel restaurant with Mum and Becca. It wasn't exactly filling. Then Mum insisted we sit down together in her room to watch a jolly musical on TV that she promised would "take our mind off things". It didn't work. We were all tense and preoccupied, and when we eventually crashed out, I couldn't get off to sleep.

I dozed fitfully and tossed and turned for ages. When I finally dropped off, I had a horrible dream about being on a rollercoaster that was out of control. I was hurtling into oblivion when I suddenly snapped wide awake.

And then I knew what was odd about the writing on the path.

S.M. WILL BE AVENGED!

*Will* be. Future tense. As if whoever was responsible for the killings hadn't finished yet.

# CROCODILE TEARS

ON our last morning, Graham and I were supposed to be Behind the Scenes in the Australian Outback. At the appointed time we set off through the almost deserted zoo.

It was a cold morning and a sharp wind cut across the grounds.

I could see at once that the keepers were worried and upset. No one was gossiping or chatting this time – they just swept cages and fed animals in grim, tight-lipped silence. You could almost taste fear hanging in the air. There was an atmosphere of anticipation – as if something even more dreadful was going to happen.

Charlie's death had changed everything. There'd

been a kind of excitement following Mr Monkton's murder – a certain level of satisfaction. OK, so the police didn't think the keepers were involved, but he hadn't been a popular man. No one on the staff had seemed bothered about him being killed.

Except one.

We were walking through the African Savannah, where Mike Hobson was mucking out the hippos, when we saw April coming towards us, heels clicking purposefully on the tarmac. She stopped, called Mike over and asked him briskly, "Have you seen Mark?"

Mike pulled his shoulders back as if he was standing to attention before replying politely, "No, I'm afraid not. Not this morning. Sorry, ma'am."

She gave a small sigh of irritation and nodded briefly at Mike, who then went back to work as if he'd been dismissed by his commanding officer. She walked on, snapping a curt "Good morning" at us as she passed by.

She was the walking embodiment of an efficient, respected boss. Which was odd, considering she was Mr Monkton's secretary. Interesting, I thought. Very interesting.

"April," I said to Graham, "was the only person who cried about Mr Monkton."

"Is that significant?" he asked.

"Maybe." I remembered her face when she'd come running back from the Frozone. She'd looked terrible. Her shock and distress had seemed genuine. But could she have been acting? "There's something funny about her," I said. I stopped and looked back towards the house – a vast stately home with acres and acres of land. It must be worth a fortune.

"What will happen to it all?" I wondered aloud. "Who will inherit this lot?"

Graham frowned. "An estate would normally pass to the next of kin."

"Next of kin?"

"The wife or children – or, failing that, the nearest surviving relative. It said in the information I downloaded that Mr Monkton's brother was killed in a car accident some years ago. It will probably go to a nephew or niece," said Graham. "Seeing as he never married."

"As far as we know," I said.

"What are you suggesting?" asked Graham, surprised.

"April…" I said slowly as I finally realized what had been odd about her manner. "When we first saw her with Mr Monkton she was formal and polite, wasn't she? Like any secretary would be with their boss. She called him 'sir', and she was like that at the party, too, once the staff began to arrive. But in the entrance hall

– when she thought no one was around – she called him 'dear', do you remember? She straightened his tie. And she picked fluff off his jacket. That's the kind of thing you only do if you're close to someone." I grabbed Graham by the arm. "Suppose she was married to him? She'd inherit the lot!"

"Surely people would know if they'd been married. No one's said anything about it."

"They might have done it in secret."

"Why would they have done that?" asked Graham.

"He was really rich!" I exclaimed, setting off once more. "And you know what families can be like about money. I bet his relatives would have objected if they'd known he was planning to marry his secretary. Especially with him being a bit eccentric. They'd have called her a gold-digger or something."

Graham glanced at me with rising excitement. "As you know, money and property are number five on the motives for murder list."

"So it's possible that April could have persuaded him to marry her and then killed him off? The whole 'S.M.' thing could be a diversion?"

Graham nodded eagerly. "It's certainly plausible. But would she have had time to stab him? She wasn't gone very long. And where does Charlie Bales fit in?"

I thought some more. "OK... Here's what I think

could have happened," I said at last. "We were right about Charlie. He did fake the sickness and sneak out to stab Mr Monkton. April could have been paying him to do it. But then he got too pushy. Perhaps he started threatening to blackmail her or something – that's just the kind of thing he'd have been likely to do, isn't it? He'd probably have thought it was all a big joke. So she had to get rid of him."

By then we'd reached the Australian Outback. We'd arrived five minutes early for our session, so we stopped to draw breath, leaning on a fence overlooking the enclosure where an enormous saltwater crocodile lay basking under a sun-lamp.

"Sadly, we don't have a single shred of evidence. Do you think we ought to mention it to the police anyway?" asked Graham.

I didn't answer. Because it was then that I noticed the shoe wedged between the rocks to one side of the crocodile. My stomach turned over.

Kids lose shoes all the time. They're forever pulling them off and throwing them out of their pushchairs before their parents notice. It's not remotely unusual to see a toddler's sandal or trainer all on its own.

But this wasn't a kid's shoe. It was an adult's. Black leather. Laces. A quality shoe; the kind that wouldn't get lost easily or by accident. And it was excessively shiny. I had a horrible feeling that I'd seen that shoe somewhere before.

Just then, a keeper came banging through the door marked STAFF ONLY, talking angrily into his walkie-talkie.

"Is Mark with you?" he demanded.

"No," Kylie's voice crackled faintly back. She sounded close to tears. "He was supposed to be checking the monkey's abscess first thing. His bag's here but he's gone and vanished on me."

"If you see him, tell him to hurry up. I've got a wallaby that needs looking at. I've been waiting ages for him."

I looked at the shoe again and then at the crocodile. Its stomach seemed tight as a drum; its smile really very self-satisfied. Just how big a breakfast had it eaten?

Mark: the vet whose name Mr Monkton had forgotten at the staff party. April had been looking for him. Kylie had said he'd vanished. I began to suspect that Graham and I had just found him.

# THE WRITING ON THE WALL

**S.M.** Vengeance brings freedom!

The words were daubed in red paint on the far side of the crocodile enclosure. Graham and I hadn't been able to see them where we'd been standing, but right after we'd called the police and they'd arrived in a storm of blue flashing lights and screaming sirens, Inspector Murray had spotted them straight away.

April had come hurrying back from the office and practically collapsed on the path when Inspector Murray pointed the writing out to her. Her grief seemed to be one hundred per cent genuine. Or perhaps she was a very good actress.

Our gruesome discovery meant that Mum had to be

called away once again so that Inspector Murray could interview us in a corner of the hotel lobby. She'd been immersed in a vat of Volcanic Mud when they plucked her out of the spa, and by the time the policeman had finished with us it had pretty much hardened. She was cracking up. Literally.

"You two are to stay right here in the hotel," she told us as soon as Inspector Murray had left. "Go upstairs and pack your stuff. Don't you dare set a foot outside – it's far too dangerous. The second I've finished this treatment, we're leaving. This has been the most stressful weekend of my life." She headed back to the spa, leaving a trail of small, muddy chunks across the polished wooden floor. The stuff was so thick, I didn't think it would be coming off any time soon.

I reckoned we had about an hour before we'd be dragged away from the zoo. "S.M.," I said to Graham after Mum had disappeared through the doors. "I suppose it all comes down to him. Which knocks the April theory on the head. Unless she's doing it to mislead the police."

"That's a strong possibility," said Graham. "Although I can't understand why she'd want to kill the vet. I just don't see where he fits in."

"*Vengeance brings freedom,*" I murmured. "Freedom for whom? Not for anyone who knew Sandy. The keepers all looked miserable this morning. Do you reckon the protesters outside might have had something to do with it?"

"Motive. Means. Opportunity," observed Graham. "That's what we have to consider. The protesters would certainly have the motive. But as to the means and the opportunity, I'm not so sure."

"This place is open to the public. It's not like you could tell the difference between a protester and anyone else unless they were carrying a placard."

"True. But how could they have killed Mr Monkton? That happened during the staff party – the site was closed to everyone apart from them and the hotel guests."

I considered. "It's a big place. Perhaps someone came in during the day and hid until after closing time?"

"I can see why one of the protesters might want to kill Mr Monkton. But why attack Charlie – or the vet?"

"I'm not sure," I said. "I suppose it depends on how much they hate this place. Might they have killed Charlie because he was a keeper? And the vet because he worked for the zoo?"

"I gather that people can get very passionate about such causes," Graham said slowly. "But you're forgetting the writing. It seems to me that if the protesters were behind it, they'd daub something different on the walls. FREE THE CAPTIVES or something – a slogan from one of their placards. Besides, the zoo's been closed to the public for the past two days. Surely no one could have got in without being spotted?"

"Yes, you're probably right." I sighed. "So it all comes back to Sandy Milford. We need to know more about his death – not just what was in the papers. There must be more on the zoo's computers. Reports or something. It's no good, Graham. We'll have to get into their system. Quickly, before Mum finishes in the spa."

"I don't think it will be possible from the computers in our rooms."

"No, but we could try the education centre. Zara won't be there, will she? She must have fed the cockroaches by now. It's not like there'll be any kids in today. I bet she's gone off home again."

With one of his blink-and-you-miss-it grins Graham pulled his library card from his pocket. "I think we might be needing this."

Graham could open locked doors with his library card, but on this occasion we didn't need to make use of his special talent. When we crossed the courtyard to the education centre the place was already open.

The ground floor was deserted, but as soon as we entered we could hear footsteps above us. Climbing the stairs to the office we found Zara, apparently cleaning out the cupboards. She looked up, surprised, when Graham and I came in. "Hello, you two. What are you doing here?"

If Mum hadn't been about to drag us off home, I don't think I'd have said anything. We'd probably have made up some lame excuse and sneaked back later when the place was empty. But we were both desperate to find out more about Sandy Milford, and this was the last chance we were going to get. We had to grab it with both hands.

"Could we use your computer?" I asked. "We want to look something up."

"Erm... I don't know, really," she said, taken aback by the request. "Can't you use the one in your room?"

"The maids are cleaning in there," Graham lied, surprising me once again with his capacity for low cunning. "They're doing mine, too. It won't take a minute."

"I don't know if I should... It's probably against the rules." She chewed her lip anxiously for a second but then her shoulders drooped despairingly and she said, "I don't suppose it matters now. Everything's been turned upside down. All these deaths! I wish I'd never come to work here. It's been horrible from day one." She shrugged and, gesturing towards her desk, added, "Go on. Help yourselves."

Graham switched on her computer and sat down in

the swirly-whirly chair before she changed her mind. But it was going to be extremely awkward doing any research while she was in the room. Frantically, I tried to think of a way to get rid of her.

I glanced at her from beneath my fringe. Took in the lost and miserable expression on her face. She looked out of her depth; like she wanted to go to bed and hide under the duvet for a week.

"Why don't you go home?" I said soothingly. "There won't be any kids visiting today, will there?"

"No, there won't." She sighed. "I don't know why I bothered coming in at all. Just wanted to show willing, I suppose." She blew her nose.

"We won't be here very long," I wheedled. "We'll shut the door behind us when we go."

The idea of escape was too tempting for her to resist. "Yeah. Maybe you're right. I will go home. I probably shouldn't do this, but... Well, you're both sensible kids, aren't you. You will flip the catch on the door when you leave?"

"Sure."

She smiled weakly. "Bye, then."

I watched Zara disappear forlornly down the steps. When I heard the door slam shut, I turned my attention to the computer. Pulling up a wooden stool, I looked over Graham's shoulder while he typed.

It didn't take him long to find an incident report that described exactly what had happened on that fateful day.

We read it in silence. One Monday morning a year before, the zoo vet, Mark Sawyer, had been doing a routine health check of the three tiger cubs.

"Do you think those are the three big ones that are here now?" I asked. "How long does it take for a tiger to grow up?"

"I presume it takes about a year for them to reach maturity. That would be the normal rate of growth for a large carnivore, anyway. I would therefore think it's highly likely that they're the same animals."

We turned back to the report. The cubs' mother had been lured into a cage in the service area while the vet and Sandy Milford caught her babies. Not liking being handled, the cubs had started hissing and spitting at their captors. The tigress had become enraged and repeatedly thrown herself against the cage door until the rusty hinges gave way. She had sprung at Sandy, felling him with one blow of her paw before biting and killing him instantly. The vet had already pressed his panic button and the zoo's emergency response team had reacted immediately. Taking the rifle from Mr Monkton's office, Charlie Bales and his boss had sped to the tiger enclosure. When they had arrived the tigress had been between Mark Sawyer and the way out, crouching, ready to pounce. They had had no choice. As she had sprung forward, Mr Monkton had given the order and Charlie had shot the tigress in the back of the head.

Exactly where he'd been shot himself.

Goosebumps prickled down my arms when I read that part. "Is there more?" I asked. "Can you find anything else?"

Graham scrolled through all kinds of files but he couldn't find any more information about the accident. He did find something else, though. A purchase order that showed Mr Monkton was paying for a memorial stone for Sandy Milford. A large marble plaque was to be erected near the gates. His full name, Alexander Duncan Milford, was going to be on it, along with the date he died and the words *Much missed*.

I read it twice. I could feel an idea dangling almost within reach. "Alexander," I said aloud, trying to grasp it. "Not Sandy."

"No. Well, you'd only put someone's full name on a memorial stone, wouldn't you?"

"So why did the graffiti say S.M.?"

"I suppose the writer must have been someone who knew him well enough to use his nickname," said Graham reasonably.

It made sense, but I had the feeling there was more to it than that. I got off my stool and started to pace the length of the room. "All the people who have died were linked to that accident in some way. There was even that maintenance guy who killed himself. But maybe he didn't! Maybe he was murdered too…"

"He could have been. If his negligence caused the tigress to break through and kill Sandy, our murderer could well have decided to target him. But why kill the vet? It most certainly wasn't his fault."

"I don't know. We're missing something." I said nothing for a while, trying to work it out. I sat down again and cupped my head in my hands. "We thought it was to do with avenging Sandy," I said at last, "but maybe it wasn't. Maybe the keepers' alibis fitted together perfectly because they were all true. Maybe Charlie really *was* sick. I think we've been looking at it from the wrong end."

"The wrong end?" echoed Graham. "Which end should we have been looking at it from?"

"Sandy wasn't the only one to die that day, was he?" I said suddenly.

"What do you mean?"

"The tigress! Do we know anything about her?"

Graham shrugged. "If we're right in assuming that she was the mother of the present three tigers, we know that she was Sumatran. That's the smallest of the existing sub-species of tiger. Highly endangered, of course."

"Sumatran," I echoed. A thought tickled at the back of my brain. "Did she have a name?"

We looked back at the report, and there it was. I'd been so interested in the people, I'd skipped over that piece of information. And it was the key to the whole thing. My heart was thumping with excitement as I read aloud, *"Sumatran Maharani."* I looked at Graham. "S.M."

His mouth dropped open.

"How could we have been so *stupid*?" I exclaimed. *"She* was the one being avenged, not Sandy Milford! It's been about her all along."

"So who did it?" asked Graham.

"I don't know. But I reckon those protesters must have something to do with it. An innocent tiger being shot by its jailers? That's what they'd say, isn't it? It certainly gives them plenty to be angry about."

"So ... if it's to do with the tigress," said Graham, "we need to know more about her." He turned back to the computer. "She must be here somewhere. They're part of a captive breeding scheme, according to the sign on the cage. There must be records about her."

It didn't take long for Graham to find out that

Sumatran Maharani had been sent to Farleigh Manor from Grampian Zoo.

"Grampian?" Something stirred deep in my memory. "Didn't Kylie say that someone there was killed by an elephant?"

"Yes," said Graham, frowning. He scrolled down and then murmured, "Here we are. He was called Dougal McTaggart, the director of Grampian Zoo. Which just so happens to be where Sumatran Maharani was born."

"Another accident? Or do you reckon he might have been murdered too? It's got to be connected with what's been happening here, hasn't it?"

"The chances of it being purely coincidental are very slim," said Graham as he accessed the Grampian Zoo website. He couldn't find anything, so he typed "Grampian Zoo Sumatran tigers" into the search engine and came up with an entry that had been posted five years ago. It was about a tiger cub that was being hand-reared by a keeper called Chris Ball.

"Chris?" I gasped. "Those protesters called the ferret-faced guy Christopher! Could it be him?"

"Possibly." Graham looked at me. "From what Kylie said, we know that hand-rearing requires an awful lot of dedication. Regular feeds several times a night. You wouldn't get a proper night's sleep for months on end."

"You'd have to really love animals to do that, wouldn't you?" I said. "Can you find a picture of this Chris person?"

For several nail-biting minutes Graham drew a blank. But eventually he found an old photograph in the archives of a Scottish paper. The hair was dark, not orange, but the smiling face of the keeper holding the tiny cub was unmistakeable. Chris Ball wasn't the ferret-featured man from the gates.

It was Zara.

# VENGEANCE BRINGS FREEDOM!

"CHRISTINE, not Christopher," I said, staring at the computer. "Wow."

In front of us Zara's face grinned happily from the screen.

Then, behind us, the real-life version came back through the door – and she was neither grinning nor happy. She hadn't left the building at all. She'd listened to our entire conversation. Her depressed, ditzy manner had completely vanished. Her features were hard. Determined. And she was carrying a gun.

"How very reckless of you," she said grimly, pointing the rifle in our direction. "You seem to have worked it all out."

"Revenge," I told her flatly. "Starting with Dougal McTaggart." I stared at her for a moment and then said angrily, "It's an awful lot of people to kill for one tiger."

"You don't understand," she said, glaring at me with hate-filled eyes. "No one does. She's dead because those stupid people let her down. I loved Maharani. She was mine. Mine!" Zara jabbed the butt of her rifle at the computer screen. It smashed to the floor and died with an eerie electronic whine. "I looked after her from the day she was born. She was so weak, so fragile. The vet said she wouldn't survive. He wanted to put her down. I wouldn't let him. Night after night I sat up with her, willing her to live. And she did. For me. She was so special. So precious! But Dougal just treated her like any other animal. When she was old enough he sent her off for breeding. I begged him not to, but he insisted. He persuaded Mr Monkton to take her. I pleaded for a transfer so I could go with her. I knew she'd be miserable without me. But he wouldn't listen. And then they shot her."

"So you killed Dougal McTaggart?"

"Yes. It was easy enough to arrange an accident. That elephant used to be in a circus, so she was very good at following orders. I only had to say the word. Alisha stepped back, and that was it."

"And then what?" I demanded. "You tried to get a job here?"

"Yes. It took a while: there weren't any vacancies for keepers. So when I saw a post advertised in the education centre, I changed my name, faked a CV and got the job. Then I plotted my revenge."

"Archie Henshaw? Was he your second victim?" asked Graham.

"Archie? Ah yes, him. Did he jump or was he pushed?" Her lips curled into a malicious smile. "Pushed."

"But why?"

"He didn't do his job properly. If his workmanship had been better, Maharani would never have broken through."

"Is that how you killed Mark Sawyer, too?" I demanded. "Pushed him into the enclosure?"

"It wasn't difficult. I told him there was an emergency with the crocodile. A blow to the head first thing this morning and he toppled straight over the wall. Easy. Served him right. If he hadn't wanted to look at Maharani's cubs in the first place, she would still be alive."

"And you shot Charlie," I said.

"Naturally." Zara smiled again. "With the same gun he used on Maharani. I'd say that was poetic justice, wouldn't you? They keep it in Mr Monkton's office. In a locked cabinet, of course, but I took the key from him before I killed him."

"But that's not right." Graham shook his head indignantly. "You might have committed all those other murders, but you *couldn't* have killed Mr Monkton. We saw you! You were in that teddy-bear suit being chased around all evening."

Zara looked from Graham to me and back again, her eyebrows raised like a teacher waiting for the correct answer. And suddenly I saw exactly how she'd done it.

Cursing myself for my slowness I said, "It wasn't you, was it? Someone else was in that suit."

She didn't say anything.

Suddenly the ferrety features of the protester at the gates came into my mind. "That man. Christopher. Were you working with him?"

Zara nodded slowly. "Well done. I bumped into him in the supermarket one night. We got talking. When I told him what I was planning, it wasn't difficult to persuade him to help. I hid him in the boot of my car when I came back for the party that night. Christopher wore the teddy-bear suit while I despatched Mr Monkton."

"But all those stab wounds... I thought lots of different people must have done it."

Zara gave a short, sharp laugh. "Did you? How fanciful. It wouldn't have been like that if the wretched man had stood still. He would keep moving! It made things a little messy."

"Poor Mr Monkton," I whispered sadly. "He felt so guilty! He hated giving the order to shoot. He had nightmares about it."

"And you think I don't?" Zara spat.

"Charlie had to do it," I protested. "Maharani was going to kill the vet."

"So what? Why do you assume that people are more important than animals? Maharani was protecting her cubs. Doing what a mother should do. Why did she have to die for it?" Zara's eyes gleamed with savage fury. "It's too late to save her, but I'm going to save her cubs."

"What are you going to do?"

"I'm taking them away. Now. While everyone's attention is on the crocodile enclosure. The police are so busy on the other side of the zoo, no one will notice what I'm up to here."

Graham looked intrigued. "Are you going to put them back in the wild? Only I'd have thought that with deforestation their chances of survival might be slim."

"The wild?" Zara echoed incredulously. "Of course not! They wouldn't stand a chance! I'm taking them to where they'll be safe. There are plenty of people who don't think animals should be held in zoos for the public to gawp at. I've decided to make use of them.

Some have a lot of money, including Christopher. He's got room for them on his country estate." Zara checked her watch. "He'll be bringing the lorry in right now."

"He won't get past the gatekeeper!" Graham protested. "Ron Baker won't let him in."

"Yes, he will. Christopher will be in disguise. And I've told Ron I'm expecting a delivery of new seating for the education centre. He won't bat an eyelid." Zara clicked the safety catch off the gun and took a step forward so the end was now pressing into my chest. "You can come with me."

"What are you planning to do with us?" I tried but failed to keep the tremble out of my voice.

"What better way to lure my tigers into the lorry than with a bit of live bait? It brings the concept of environmental enrichment to a whole new level."

"You wouldn't really feed a pair of children to the tigers, would you?" Graham's words came out as high and squeaky as mine.

"After those Brownies?" Zara laughed nastily. "Believe me, I've had enough of kids to last me a lifetime."

Mum and Becca were still stuck in the mud. The zoo was empty. We walked to the Rainforest without seeing a single other human being. No one even came within shouting distance. They were all watching the police combing through the crocodile enclosure so they could find out how Mark Sawyer had met his grisly end.

When we reached the tigers, Christopher, dressed in a nondescript boiler suit with a realistic fake beard, was already there. I thought the sight of two kids being forced along at gunpoint would make him uneasy; I hoped we might be able to appeal to his better nature. But clearly he didn't have one. When Zara muttered "bait" to him, he merely nodded and stood aside to let us pass.

Christopher had already backed his lorry through the wooden gates and parked it in the service area. Zara ordered Graham and me to climb up into a barred travelling cage in the back and then flipped a series of levers and catches that connected it to one of the tunnels. Then she opened the first gate through to the tigers' enclosure.

There was nothing we could do. She had a gun: we'd be dead if we tried anything. The only escape route was through the tunnel, into the tiger cage. For a moment I considered it, but only for a moment. Because then Zara was banging on the side of a bucket filled with slabs of steak and the three tigers were stalking slowly, elegantly into the holding pen. The gate clanged shut behind them. Zara slid open the door to the tunnel and threw a piece of meat into it to encourage them forward. They were in. The door closed. They could only go forward. We could feel the weight of them as they approached, and the iron mesh of the tunnel creaked and groaned. The lorry swayed with each step. They were coming. Towards us. Graham was fumbling with his phone, trying to call for help, but his hands were stiff and awkward. He was terrified. He dropped it. It fell through the wire, through a gap in the floorboards and shattered on the concrete below. My legs gave way. I sank down. Put my hands over my eyes. Like an ostrich burying its head in the sand, I didn't want to see what happened next. I just hoped it would be over quickly. There was nothing between us and the tigers. Nowhere to hide. No hope of survival. I opened my fingers and peered through the crack. For a split second I stared into a pair of wild amber eyes. Hot, carnivorous breath was on my face. A sandpaper tongue rasped against my head. I was dead meat. Literally.

But then the tiger turned and sniffed the air. Zara was outside the lorry, still holding the bucket of steak. The tigers weren't used to live food; they preferred ready meals. The one who'd licked me sniffed the air again. Looked at the bucket. Batted at the side of the mesh, trying to get to it. And the workmanship on the cage was as bad as Archie Henshaw's. Shoddy. Badly maintained. The rusty catches gave way.

Three tigers spilled out of the lorry. The bucket was knocked from Zara's hand as they each seized a chunk of meat.

It might have been all right. There was a moment when things could have been OK. If Zara had thrown more food into another pen, she could have re-caught them and got away unharmed. But then Christopher screamed. High and loud. Like Mr Monkton. And the tigers hated it.

A snarl.

A growl of warning.

*Thud!* One blow from a paw and Christopher would never scream again.

And the tigers were still upset. Quarrelsome. Fighting over what was left of the raw meat. They turned their attention to Zara. She had the gun, she could have saved herself, but Zara wouldn't shoot. Not a tiger.

She dropped the rifle, which clattered on the concrete as she opened her arms wide. She looked as if she was inviting a kitten to jump onto her lap. And one of them did jump – but its claws were unsheathed, its jaw agape. For a split second I saw the glint of those teeth flashing in the sun, then I shut my eyes. Graham and I hung on to each other in the back of that lorry, trying to make ourselves invisible. And then it was over.

Kylie had heard Christopher's scream and come running. Zara might have stolen the rifle from Mr Monkton's office, but the vet had left his bag in Kylie's kitchen and there was a tranquillizer gun in it. She didn't even radio for help: she climbed straight up on the roof and darted the tigers.

Waiting for them to fall asleep was the scariest bit, as far as Graham and I were concerned. It was only a few minutes but it seemed to take for ever. In the meantime we had to remain still and silent, desperately hoping that the tigers wouldn't come for us. We were extremely pleased when they finally toppled over, but also extremely pleased that they hadn't been killed. By that time we'd seen more than enough death.

There's not much to add, really. It turned out we'd been right about April. She *had* married Mr Monkton, and – despite a legal challenge from one of his nephews – she did inherit the whole place. But she ran it well, and although she kept the yurts and the hotel as a tribute to her late husband, she put all her energy into sprucing up the zoo. They built this huge new aquarium with sharks and coral reefs and walk-through tanks, which won a really big conservation award. By the time it opened, Kylie and Pete had got together and

Sandy's wife had gone back to work at the zoo because their youngest kid had started school. I knew perfectly well that the keepers would be supporting each other. Zara hadn't lied about that – they really were a close, tight-knit group. I was glad to hear they were all getting on OK. But when our teacher organized a school trip to Farleigh Manor, Graham and I decided not to go along. We'd experienced enough of the Animal Kingdom to last us both a lifetime.